Acknowledgments:
Models made by Humphrey Leadbitter for Whoopee! Productions Limited
Backgrounds illustrated by Martin Aitchison

British Library Cataloguing in Publication Data
Hately, David
   Rupert and the magic seeds.
   I. Title
   823′.914 [J]
   ISBN 0-7214-1217-3

First edition

Published by Ladybird Books Ltd Loughborough Leicestershire UK
Ladybird Books Inc Auburn Maine 04210 USA

Printed in England

RUPERT
and the
Magic Seeds

Based on an original story
Rupert and the Worg Seeds by James Henderson
Adapted by David Hately

Ladybird Books

One April day, the
Nutwood postman
brought a parcel to
Rupert's door. It was
from an aunt and
uncle who lived in a
far-off land across the sea.

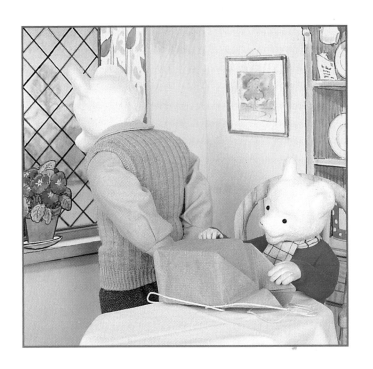

"**T**hese are supposed to be our Christmas presents," said Mr Bear. "But everything's late this year." He sighed as he looked out of the window at the wintry garden. "It's April already, and there's no sign of spring yet! It still feels like winter."

But Rupert was more interested in the parcel than in the garden.

Inside the parcel were some packets of flower seeds for Mr Bear, a necklace made of dried seeds for Mrs Bear, and a brightly painted wooden object, shaped like an Easter egg, for Rupert.

A letter wished everyone
a happy Christmas
and explained that
Rupert's present
was a musical rattle.

Rupert shook it. It made a soft, dry,
rattling noise. "I can use this in the
school orchestra,"
he said.

Next day, Rupert noticed that the plug on the end of the rattle was loose.

He started to push it back into place, but then decided to see what made the rattling sound.

He took the plug out and peered into the little hole, but it was too dark to see anything. Holding it up over his head, he tilted it to get a better view.

Two little seeds dropped out and, before he could stop himself, Rupert swallowed them.

Rupert ran straight to his mummy and asked her to fetch the doctor. "I've just swallowed some very strange seeds!" he cried.

But, to everyone's dismay, by the time Dr Lion arrived, Rupert had begun to shrink! The doctor examined the rest of the seeds in Rupert's rattle.

"These are *worg* seeds," he said at last. "Their name is the opposite of *grow*. Don't worry, Rupert! You'll be back to full size in a couple of days."

But by the next morning, Rupert had shrunk to the size of a toy soldier and Mrs Bear had to make him some new clothes.

The tiny bear sat watching his father work in the icy garden. Then, feeling bored, he crept down the path to look out through the garden gate.

Suddenly a huge bird
swooped down on
him! It was only a
jackdaw, but it
gripped Rupert by
his jersey and
carried him out
of the garden.

The bird dropped Rupert into its nest high up in a hole in an old wall and then flew off again.

Rupert looked round at the treasures the jackdaw had collected. They included a thimble, some nails, a broken comb and a ball of wool.

The wool gave Rupert an idea. He knotted one end to a strong twig overhanging the nest and threw the ball of wool over the edge of the nest. Then he made his escape by climbing down the woollen rope. But when he was halfway down, the wool snapped!

Rupert landed with a bump on the grass. But, to his horror, the ground gave way beneath him! He tumbled through a trapdoor and found himself falling down a shaft.

Rupert grabbed at a rope ladder that was fixed to the wall of the shaft. He heard a loud CLANG as the trapdoor above him slammed shut.

Rupert climbed back up the ladder. As he did so he noticed that the ladder was just the right size for him. "So whoever lives down here is small, like me!" he said to himself.

But try as he might, Rupert couldn't open the trapdoor. It was shut tight. Below him he could see a glowing light. There was nothing for it but to climb down and explore.

At the bottom of the shaft Rupert
found a brightly lit passage. At the
end of the passage there was a small
wooden door.

Now although Rupert wanted to find a way out of the underground cave, he was curious to know what lay behind the door. There might be someone there who could help him.

He listened at the door, and wondered whether to go in.

Something on the other side of the door was making a strange noise! It sounded like a sigh, followed by a snorty kind of rumble. *Sigh, snort, rumble. Sigh, snort, rumble. Sigh, snort, rumble.*

Then Rupert remembered that his father made the same kind of noise when he took a nap in front of the fire with the newspaper over his face. It was the sound of SNORING.

Carefully, he turned the handle and opened the door. He found himself in a room with lots of beds, and in each one there was a little imp, snoring.

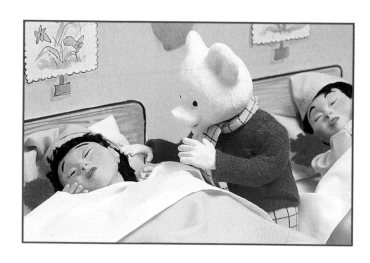

Rupert recognised the little creatures at once. They were the Imps of Spring! It was their job to wake up the countryside after its long winter sleep.

"No wonder it still feels like winter outside," cried Rupert. "The Imps have overslept!"

Rupert raced to the other end of the room. There, in the largest bed of all, was an Imp wearing a crown.

"Wake up!" cried Rupert, shaking the King Imp. "It's half-past spring!"

The King Imp jumped out of bed and dashed round the room waking the sleeping Imps.

"We can't thank you enough," he told Rupert. "But how did you find us?"

Rupert told the Imps about the worg seeds, and how the jackdaw had carried him off.

"Don't worry, Rupert," said the King Imp. "We'll take you back to Nutwood."

Mr and Mrs Bear were overjoyed to have Rupert home, safe and sound.

As he tucked into his supper he told them all about his adventures with the Imps of Spring.

T he next day, Rupert was back to his normal size again. Outside the air felt much warmer and Mr Bear went into the garden to plant his seeds.

Rupert put his rattle containing the worg seeds on a shelf. "I've had enough trouble with seeds to last me a very long time!" he said.

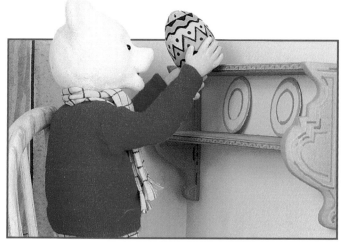